1 to 10
Count Again

A GOLDEN BOOK • NEW YORK
Western Publishing Company, Inc., Racine, Wisconsin 53404

These babies have a busy day
Counting things as they play.

1

Baby Mickey's just begun.
He's looking for the number 1!

2

Baby Minnie's boats are blue.
She can count them—1 and 2.

3

Baby Pete says, "Look at me!"
He's made some mud pies—1, 2, 3.

Baby Donald sees it pour
And counts the puddles near the door.
1, 2, 3, 4.

5 Baby Mickey's planes can dive.
He can count them up to five.
1, 2, 3, 4, 5.

6

Baby Daisy wants to fix
A home for all her baby chicks.
1, 2, 3, 4, 5, 6.

7

Baby Minnie likes to play
With her doll whose name is Kevin.
Cookies are their snack today—
1, 2, 3, 4, 5, 6, 7.

8

Baby Pluto just can't wait
To eat the biscuits on his plate.
1, 2, 3, 4, 5, 6, 7, 8.

9

Baby Goofy's new cars shine.
Can you count them? (There are nine!)
1, 2, 3, 4, 5, 6, 7, 8, 9.

10

Baby Pete is happy when
He digs flowers up again.
1, 2, 3, 4, 5, 6, 7, 8, 9, 10.

Counting is fun.
Let's count again!
Count babies' things from 1 to 10.

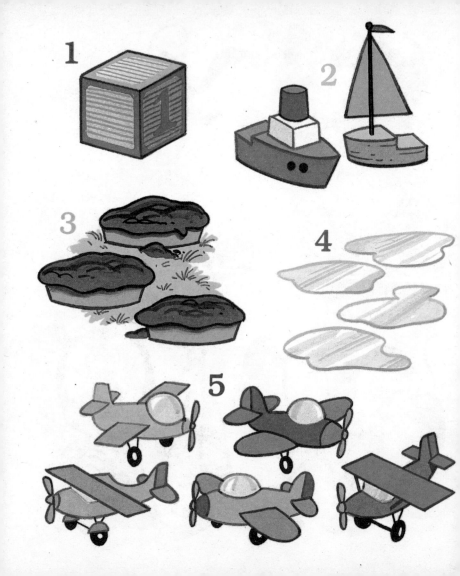